GREAT GOAL!

Rob Childs

Illustrated by Michael Reid

For My Great Mum!

GREAT GOAL!
A CORGI PUPS BOOK : 9780552568784

First published in Great Britain by Corgi Pups,
An imprint of Random House Children's Books
A Random House Group Company

Corgi Pups edition published 2001

5 7 9 10 8 6

Set in Bembo MT Schoolbook

Corgi Pups are published by Random House Children's Books,
61–63 Uxbridge Road, London W5 5SA,
A Random House Group Company

Addresses for companies within The Random House Group Limited
can be found at: www.randomhouse.co.uk/offices.htm

THE RANDOM HOUSE GROUP Limited Reg. No. 954009
www.kidsatrandomhouse.co.uk

A CIP catalogue record for this book is available from the British Library.

The Random House Group Limited supports The Forest Stewardship
Council® (FSC®), the leading international forest-certification organisation.
Our books carrying the FSC label are printed on FSC®-certified paper.
FSC is the only forest-certification scheme supported by the leading
environmental organisations, including Greenpeace. Our
paper procurement policy can be found at
www.randomhouse.co.uk/environment

MIX
Paper from
responsible sources
FSC® C018072

Printed and bound in Great Britain by Clays Ltd, St Ives plc

Contents

Series Reading Consultant: Prue Goodwin,
Reading and Language Information Centre,
University of Reading

Chapter One

"You can't miss!"

Strawberry proved the captain wrong. No sooner had Tom's cry left his lips than the striker lofted the ball over the crossbar.

"Oh, brilliant!" Tom sneered.
"First chance we get to score
and you go and blast the ball
into orbit."

"Not my fault,"
mumbled
Strawberry,
blushing as red as the fruit that
gave Stephen Berry his nick-
name. "It must have hit a bump
or something."

The village recreation ground
may not have boasted the
flattest surface in the world, but
it was the only open space in
Great Catesby big enough for
an eleven-a-side game. Their
own school playing field was far
too small.

The captain was in no mood for excuses. "I notice the bumps haven't stopped them scoring four goals," he muttered.

Things might well have been a lot worse if Hannah had not been on top form in goal, and she was soon in the thick of the action again. The keeper dived

bravely among the flying boots
in a goalmouth scramble to
wrap her body around the ball.

Imran tapped her gently on
the shoulder. "OK, it's safe to get
up now," the defender said.
"They've all gone . . ."

Hannah uncurled herself like
a cat waking up from a nap in
front of the fire.

". . . But they'll soon be
back," Imran added with a grin.

"Well, what do you expect?" she said, giving a shrug. "I mean, it's not that they're so much better than us. They're just bigger – and older."

"Well saved, Hannah," called out their teacher, Mrs Roberts, who was in charge of the practice match between the school's two junior classes. "Now let's see how far you can kick it."

Hannah booted the ball away
as hard as she could. It still fell
well short of the halfway line,
but at least found a teammate
on the left wing.

Rebecca hadn't touched the ball for ages and she wasn't going to waste this chance to play with it. The winger beat the first defender for sheer pace and then used her dribbling skills to outwit the second.

"Yes, Becky – to me!" cried Tom, running up in support.

Rebecca ignored him. She tried to dribble her way past another player instead, but the tackle was too strong and the ball was lost.

"That was greedy!" Tom complained. "You should have passed."

Rebecca made no reply. She knew the captain was right.

All was forgotten and forgiven, however, a few minutes later, when Tom's team put together the best move of the match – with Rebecca supplying the final pass to their leading scorer, Jonty Fox.

Jonty flicked the ball up into the air and then volleyed it goalwards as it dropped. The keeper barely even saw the guided missile zoom past him.

It was their one moment of glory in the game. By the time Mrs Roberts called a halt, the score was 7–1 to the Top Juniors.

Tom slumped down wearily in the centre-circle. "Oh, well," he sighed. "Guess things can only get better . . ."

Chapter Two

Two days later, the headteacher had some wonderful news for the young children of Great Catesby.

"We've won!" Miss Jackson announced in assembly. "Thanks to all your marvellous efforts, our lovely little school is now saved!"

The children clapped and
cheered. The village school had
been in danger of closure until
the success of their recent
money-raising activities. The last
thing they'd wanted was to be
bussed into the nearby town of
Kilthorpe to attend the big
school there.

"Let's sing our special song to celebrate," said Miss Jackson.

This was the song that the pupils had recorded with a famous pop star, the Red Fox – otherwise known to them as Jonty's dad.

They didn't even wait for the headteacher to reach the piano before bursting into the chorus.

"*C'mon, you Greats! C'mon, you Greats!*

Come and watch us win our games.

Come and shout out all our names.

C'mon, you Greats! C'mon, you Greats!"

"I'm glad to hear you're in such fine voice," Miss Jackson laughed, settling herself at the piano. "Because I've had a most amazing telephone call this morning. The TV people want us to appear on *Chart Chasers!*"

The children were too stunned to react at first. *Chart Chasers* was their favourite programme on pop music.

Then the old school building was almost in need of some emergency repair work. The huge explosion of cheers nearly blew the hall roof off!

★

The coach from Great Catesby
was delayed in the heavy
London traffic and the children
were late arriving at the
television studio.

The Red Fox was already there. "Hi, gang!" he greeted them. "Glad you made it at last. Beginning to think you might have chickened out!"

"No chance of that, Dad," Jonty laughed. "Not the Greats."

Many of his teammates,
however, and also their friends
in the school choir *were* feeling a
bit nervous. Some had even been
sick on the journey, but tried to
blame it on the swaying of the
coach.

"This is so *incredible!*" breathed Hannah, her voice almost a whisper. "I can hardly believe we're really inside the *Chart Chasers* studio."

"Magic!" exclaimed Rebecca, wide-eyed with wonder. "Have you still got butterflies in your tummy?"

The goalkeeper shook her head. "Not any more. They've all flown away now we're here, just like they do when a match kicks off."

The children had the most fantastic time over the next few hours. During breaks in rehearsals with the Red Fox's band, the Earthlings, they went round collecting the autographs of as many stars as they dared to ask.

Rebecca's book was soon full, but she couldn't get over the shock of being asked for her own autograph by the drummer of a big American band.

"Like yer single, little lady," he drawled, holding out a torn piece of paper. "D'yer play as well as yer sing?"

"You mean the drums?" said Rebecca, not sure if the man was making fun of her.

"No, I mean soccer," he replied seriously. "I'd sooner play soccer than the drums any day!"

Miss Jackson and Mrs Roberts watched from behind a screen as their pupils performed on stage in the show itself in front of the cameras.

"They sound super!" cried Mrs Roberts. "I'm so proud of them."

The headteacher beamed. "Best I've ever heard them sing. They've risen to the occasion — as always. I knew they would."

The young audience loved
the song, too, dancing and
swaying to the music under the
studio's multi-coloured, flashing
lights.

Backed by the choir, the Red
Fox sang along first with
Jonty . . .

"It's great, boy, it's great,
Feeling part of a team.
Playing towards the same goal,
Working together – sharing a
dream."

. . . and then with Rebecca . . .

"It's great, girl, it's great,
Being on the same side.
Whether we win, lose or draw,
Whatever the score — knowing we
tried."

The fans whooped and
clapped loudly when the final
chorus of the song ended and
the children felt almost in a
daze backstage afterwards.

"You were all
GREAT!" cried the
Red Fox in delight.
"With a bit of luck,
kids, I reckon we might even be
the new Christmas number one!"

Chapter Three

The Red Fox was proved right. *C'mon, you Greats* was indeed top of the charts on Christmas Day.

Tom celebrated their hit record in the best way that he knew how – by playing football. On Boxing Day he called round to Great Catesby Manor, the pop star's country home, to have some extra shooting practice with Jonty.

"Made cousin Jack watch a tape of the TV show yesterday after Christmas dinner," Tom chuckled as he set himself up for yet another shot. "He went all green."

"Perhaps he'd eaten too much turkey!" Jonty grinned.

"Jealousy, more like," Tom smirked. "Bet Jack can't wait till we play his Killers again next term so he can try and get his own back."

"It's *us* who are out for revenge," Jonty reminded him. "The Killers won the first game."

The captain pulled a face. He preferred to forget that Kilthorpe Primary School had 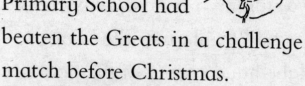 beaten the Greats in a challenge match before Christmas.

Tom belted the ball at the goal they'd drawn on a garage wall. The target was divided up into eight numbered squares, but he missed the lot.

Jonty laughed and scampered after the rebound to have his next turn. He pretended that he was taking a penalty and struck the ball firmly into the bottom right-hand corner of the goal.

"Box eight – the winner!" he cried.

"Huh! Lucky."

"Which one were you on?" Jonty asked cheekily.

"Four," he grunted. "As if you didn't know."

"Shame!" Jonty giggled. "All this fame must be going to your head."

"Watch it or I'll see this ball goes straight to yours," Tom warned him. "I sure won't miss something the size of that."

"Oh, yeah?" Jonty taunted. "You couldn't even hit a barn door."

Tom pounced on the ball and Jonty realized that the captain meant business. He ran off towards the main building, with Tom dribbling the ball after him in hot pursuit.

When Jonty slipped on a wet patch of grass on the front lawn, Tom seized his chance and let fly. He struck the ball powerfully in his stride, but Jonty saw it coming just in time and ducked out of the way.

The window wasn't so lucky.

CRASH!!

The boys stared at the broken pane of glass in horror.

"Quick, let's leg it," gasped Tom.

They weren't fast enough. The Red Fox's housekeeper came scuttling out of the front door and grabbed Jonty by the arm.

"You and your football!" she cried. "I'll see the cost of this window comes out of your pocket money, young man."

Tom resisted the natural urge to run away. "Um, actually it was my fault," he admitted. "I kicked the ball."

The woman glared at him. "Well, you can sweep up all the glass, then," she said. "Go and fetch him a brush and dustpan, Jonty."

Tom was set to work under close supervision. The house-keeper made sure every tiny piece of glass was picked up, inside and out.

Jonty couldn't resist a joke at his pal's expense. "Looks like you'd make a good sweeper!" he giggled.

Tom's face sud-denly lit up. "Hey! Thanks, Jonty," he grinned. "You've just gone and given me a wicked idea for how we might beat the Killers!"

Tom explained his new tactics to Mrs Roberts on the very first day back at school in the New Year. "You want us to change to a sweeper system?" said the teacher, looking puzzled.

"I doubt whether many of the team would know how it works. I'm not even sure that I do."

"It's worth a try, Mrs Roberts," he pleaded. "We can hardly do any worse than last time."

 "Well, that's true," she agreed, nodding. "OK, then, captain, we'll give it a go – as long as you play the role of sweeper."

Tom grinned. "Great!" he exclaimed. "I've already been getting in some practice during the holidays!"

Chapter Four

"Right, men," said Tom, addressing his mixed team of eight boys and three girls before the match. "Now we're top of the charts, let's go and show them Killers who's best at football too."

The Greats even had a full set of kit to wear at last. The Red Fox had given the school a Christmas present of six more red and white soccer strips.

The pop star was standing on the touchline as the players ran onto the Kilthorpe pitch to warm up.

"C'mon, you Greats!" he sang to greet them.

Five minutes after the kick-off, the Red Fox was jumping about even more than he did on stage.

Jonty had just put the Greats
1–0 ahead.

It was a brilliant goal.
Raspberry, Strawberry's twin
sister, slipped Jonty the ball just
outside the Killers' penalty area
and he drove it high into the
roof of the net.

The Greats did well to hold their slim lead for most of the first half. The Killers were a very good team, but it took them a long time to break down the Greats' sweeper system.

Tom had been outstanding in his new position, dealing with any passes that beat the other defenders. His favourite moment came when he swept the ball away off Jack's toes just as his cousin looked certain to score.

But even Tom could not prevent the Killers from equalizing with a header and then going 2–1 up just before half-time.

A cross from the left wing evaded Hannah's grasp and Jack had a simple tap-in goal at the far post.

"It was only a matter of time," Jack whooped. "We'll walk it now, easy!"

"No way!" Tom retorted. "The Greats never give up."

 Tom was right about that, but they still had Hannah to thank for not falling further behind straight after the break. She deflected a long-range effort against a post and then scrambled to her feet in time to smother the rebound. It was a superb double save.

As the minutes ticked by, Tom decided to push forward into midfield to try and keep the ball more in the Killers' half of the pitch. He crunched into a tackle to win the ball and curled a pass out to Rebecca.

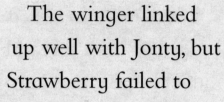

The winger linked up well with Jonty, but Strawberry failed to control her cross and the home side were able to clear the danger.

The Greats now began to dominate the match. They missed two more good chances to score, but when the equalizer finally came, it was well worth waiting for.

The Berry twins exchanged passes neatly with each other before Strawberry slid the ball forward to Rebecca.

She didn't need any more help. Glancing up, she saw the goalkeeper had advanced off his line to narrow the shooting angle. So Rebecca chipped the ball over his head instead.

Everyone watched the flight of the ball. It looked to be floating over the bar at first, but then it dipped and dropped into the top corner of the net.

"C'mon, men!" yelled Tom. "We can win this now." They did exactly that, but even Tom had to admit that he left it late. The captain was having the game of his young life, charging up and down the pitch to support both defence and attack.

And he was in the right place at the right time – the very last minute of the game – to hit the winning goal.

Rebecca's pass found him unmarked on the edge of the Killers' penalty area and Tom smacked the ball goalwards as hard as he could.

The keeper flung out an arm to try and block the shot, but it seemed almost as if he was waving the ball goodbye. It flashed into the net to make the final score 3–2 to the Greats.

The cousins shook hands after the final whistle.

"No hard feelings?" said Tom.

"No hard feelings," replied Jack, forcing a smile. "And no excuses either. You beat us fair and square today."

"Well played, everybody," said Mrs Roberts as the Greats gathered around their teacher. "I'm really proud of you."

The Red Fox joined the group too. "Great stuff, kids!" he grinned. "Happy New Year!"

They could all look forward
to a Happy New Year now and
to playing many more games of
football together as well. The
school was saved and the future
looked as bright as the Red
Fox's long red hair.

"*C'mon, you Greats!*" they sang
loudly. "*C'mon, you Greats!*"

THE END